Amber and Carter were staying with their grandmother, Nana, and their grandfather, Papa. They both enjoyed visiting without their parents. Their mother and father had dropped them off, and were going to collect them at the weekend to take them home.

On their first day, Amber, Carter, Nana, and Papa went out to the park to visit the lake. They stopped to feed the ducks, and then had an ice cream. Amber chose a vanilla cone and Carter chose a cherry one. Nana and Papa both chose the gingerbread ice cream.

Amber and Carter had never tried gingerbread ice cream before, so Nana let them try hers. They liked it so much that Nana said they should go home and bake a sticky gingerbread cake. Amber and Carter were very eager to get started, so they all walked back along the High Street.

“We need to stop and get some black treacle, some butter, and a box of eggs,” said Nana. “We also need some salad leaves and a cucumber to go with dinner.”

They got the food they needed and returned home.

Papa put the food away and then he and Nana gathered the things they would need to make the sticky gingerbread.

"Now, before we start," said Nana, "I'm going to carefully take the lid off the can of treacle and put the can on a tray, on a very, very low heat. Then we will be able to spoon it out more easily."
"We also need to clean our hands," Papa added.

“Right! First we need to line a cake pan,” said Nana, as she carefully cut some baking parchment to fit the size of the pan. “Carter, you can get a butter wrapper from the door of the fridge and rub it around the pan. That will grease it and stop the gingerbread from sticking to the sides.”

Papa got the scales out and tipped 12oz of plain flour into the bowl on the top. Amber then placed the flour into a mixing bowl while Nana found the next ingredients they would need.

"Get a teaspoon please, Carter," she said. Carter got a teaspoon and used it to add two teaspoons of bicarbonate of soda and two teaspoons of ground ginger to the bowl.

Nana took a thick teacloth and carefully took the treacle can out of the cooker. She stood it on a mat. “Be careful,” she said to Amber and Carter, “the can is quite hot.”

“We must turn up the heat now,” said Papa. “It needs to be hotter to bake the gingerbread.”

Nana took out a saucepan and put it on the counter. “Press the button so that the scales show zero,” she instructed Amber. “Time for something sweet!” They added the next ingredient to the saucepan.

“Now for the treacle,” said Nana. She took the teacloth and held the can while Amber and Carter spooned the black treacle into the pan.

The treacle was very sticky and runny. It was very difficult to get it off the spoon. Amber and Carter licked their fingers after they had wiped the treacle off the spoon.

"Now you need to clean your hands again!" chuckled Papa.

"Now we need a different sort of ginger... stem ginger," said Nana. "It is in a jar in the fridge." Papa took it out and Nana twisted off the lid. Then she told the children to get out two bulbs of ginger. "It looks completely different from the ground ginger we have cooked with before!" remarked Amber.

"Butter next," said Papa, taking it out of the fridge. "7oz."
"That will be almost the whole stick," said Nana. "We'll check that on the scales. Get the right amount and then add it to the pan. Then we need a wooden spoon to carefully stir everything until it melts. We need to keep stirring so it does not stick to the bottom of the pan and burn."

Once the butter had melted, they took the pan off the heat and left it on the counter to cool down. When the mix had cooled a bit, Nana poured it into the bowl, and Amber and Carter used wooden spoons to stir and fold in the flour and spices.

Next, Papa added 1.25 cups of milk and told Carter to beat it well, with a wooden spoon this time.
"Would you like to crack the eggs, Amber?" said Nana.
"Yes!" said Amber. "I do that at home and I'm getting good at it."

Amber gently tapped one of the eggs on the side of a mug, broke the shell, and dropped the egg into the mug. She repeated this with the other egg and then beat them together with a fork. Nana emptied the beaten eggs into the bowl and gave it a good mix.

Everyone helped to pour the gingerbread batter into the lined pan and then it was ready to bake.
"It should take just under an hour," she said.

They waited until they could smell the gingerbread, then they had a look at it. It had risen up and turned dark and golden. When Nana touched the middle it felt firm.
"That looks ready," she said. "Do you see? The edges of the gingerbread have shrunk away from the edges of the pan."

They left the tin on the counter to cool.
"It looks yummy!" said Carter.
"Yes, we can have a slice for tea," said Papa, "and, as it keeps well, we can offer some to your mother and father when they come to pick you up."

"Gingerbread was your father's favorite when he was your age, so we will need to save him a big slice!" smiled Nana, as she cut them all a slice each.